Fighting for Freedom!

SRA

Columbus, OH

SRAonline.com

 SRA

Send all inquiries to this address:
SRA/McGraw-Hill
4400 Easton Commons
Columbus, OH 43219

ISBN: 978-0-07-608799-0
MHID: 0-07-608799-9

1 2 3 4 5 6 7 8 9 NOR 13 12 11 10 09 08 07

Tilly's bare feet kicked up dust as she bolted into the cabin. She just heard the terrible news. "The old master has died! Mr. Nash owns us now!"

Mr. Nash wanted to sell some of the slaves. He planned to divide Tilly's family. Tilly, her sister Kess, and her mother were being sold to a Georgia plantation owner. Her father and her brother Nat would stay in Maryland.

Tilly's mother felt despair at the thought of being separated from her husband and son. Eli hugged his wife to comfort her. Tilly gazed at Kess and Nat asleep in a bed of straw.

The night before the slave auction, Tilly could not sleep. Worried about the future, she tossed and turned in the dark night. After midnight, an owl hooted five times somewhere close by. The haunting sound made Tilly shiver in the cool spring night. Her father sat up.

Just then an elderly woman appeared in their doorway. "Time to leave," she told Eli.

Eli smiled as he introduced their guest. "This is Moses, come to set her people free."

Tilly sucked in her breath. She knew Moses was another name for Harriet Tubman.

Tubman had once been enslaved herself, but she escaped north to freedom. She frequently returned to Maryland to help slaves escape.

Tubman was careful on these dangerous missions. Laws allowed masters to take captured slaves back.

Tilly's family crept through the darkness using the moon as their light, and Tubman as their guide.

Observing the frightened family Tubman said, "Listen closely, for this is my creed. There is one of two things I have a right to, liberty or death. If I cannot have one, I would rather have the other."

Under cover of darkness, the family followed Tubman for miles. Before long, Tubman pointed upward to the starry night.

"The North Star guides us to freedom!"

"If the night is cloudy, will we get lost?" Tilly asked.

Tubman smiled. "We follow the river. I've traveled this way many times now."

Up close, Tilly realized that Tubman was really a young woman wearing an old woman's disguise. The disguise hid her real identity. There were large rewards

for anyone who captured Tubman.

Slaves had to have a pass to allow them to leave the farm. These restrictions were made to keep slaves from running away. Returning captured slaves back to their masters was common.

They walked all night and hid during the day in the woods. Bloodhounds baying in the distance meant patrols were hunting them.

Tubman pulled a bottle from her sack. When she opened it, a sickening odor erupted from the bottle. Tubman smeared the oily substance on everyone's feet. "This will keep the dogs from smelling our tracks," she explained.

They ran to the river and quickly crossed it. Tilly no longer heard the bloodhounds. They walked until dawn, and Tubman led them to the back door of a large house.

A white woman answered their knock. Tilly wondered whether the woman would turn them in.

Without uttering a sound, the woman handed them gardening tools. Tubman began working in the garden. Tilly and her family followed and began working.

Ruth frowned as she tended the fertile soil. "Why are we working instead of resting?" Tilly's mother asked. "Kess is exhausted."

"We are helping Mrs. Larson," said Tubman, "and she is helping us. No one will suspect that we're hiding in plain sight. We are simply slaves working."

Later, Mrs. Larson provided them with food and a place to sleep until her husband came home.

Mr. Larson hid them in a crowded wagon and then drove to the next safe house, which was in Delaware.

Many freed African Americans lived in Delaware. However, the state still allowed slavery. Runaways had to be very careful. They could be arrested or captured by slave catchers.

Many people were angered by the laws that allowed masters to take slaves back. These people were known as abolitionists. The Larsons were abolitionists who helped runaway slaves. Abolitionists helped form the Underground Railroad.

Freedom would not be a luxury that Tilly's family knew until they reached Canada.

Tubman led them to many safe houses, following the Underground Railroad. Some abolitionists used secret codes and signs when helping runaways.

Pointing to a lantern on a hitching post outside a home, Tubman explained, "We enter this house safely. A missing lantern means danger."

Traveling on, they reached Philadelphia, Pennsylvania, the most overwhelming city Tilly had seen. Overcrowded streets made crossing them difficult.

"I need to raise money to get to Canada," Tubman explained. "Be careful because Philadelphia has many slave catchers."

Kess clung to Ruth, shaking.

"Don't worry," Ruth whispered. "Freedom awaits."

"I'm a conductor," Tubman said. "On my Underground Railroad, I never run my locomotive off the track, and I've never lost a passenger."

"It's not a real locomotive," said Nat.

"No," his father agreed, "but it is taking us to our destination."

While they waited, Tilly and her family met some of Tubman's friends. One was Fredrick Douglass, a freed African American, who was from Maryland, near Tilly's old home.

Another, William Still, was a freeborn African American who could read and write. He kept a journal on fugitive slaves.

Eventually, Tubman raised enough money to take a real train to Buffalo, New York. Tilly was excited, but uneasy about the trip.

Tilly and her family hurried onto the station platform. Smoke belched from the locomotive's engine. The conductor led them to the baggage car.

The train lurched forward, throwing Tilly against a packing crate. It headed north. Everyone clung to something sturdy as the train picked up speed. The baggage car swayed gently, rocking Kess to sleep. Dreams of freedom kept Tilly awake. In Canada they would be refugees. She had fled slavery for protection in another country.

They had been traveling for more than a month now. Their nerves were on edge from always having to be alert to danger.

Tilly knew little about Canada, except that it was cold. Tilly laughed. She would happily face the cold to be free.

Life was already new and different. She had real clothes, instead of a potato-sack dress. She owned a pair of shoes, and they felt strange on her feet.

Days later, they arrived in Buffalo, New York. "We're almost there!" Tilly exclaimed as they stepped off the train. "We're almost free!"

"You're free now," Tubman said, "but you won't be safe until we cross the Niagara River."

The weary travelers walked to the Niagara River and admired the breathtaking falls. Then, they walked farther to the handmade suspension bridge leading to Canada. The bridge swayed, making Tilly gulp with fear, but Tubman did not hesitate. Tilly swallowed her fear and followed.

In the middle of the bridge, Tubman said, "You are free now."

Nat said, "So we're no longer slaves?"

Eli laughed. "We are slaves to no one."

Tilly felt an overwhelming sense of joy. Leaning over the bridge handrail, she yelled, "I'm not a slave anymore! I'm free! I'm safe! I'm—" Words could not express her jubilation.

For the last time, Tilly's family followed Tubman. She stepped onto Canada's shoreline and said, "Now you will have freedom and liberty."

Ruth dropped to her knees and kissed the ground, and sighed. "What will I do with all this liberty?"

Tubman smiled. "I grew up like a neglected weed—ignorant of liberty, having no experience in it. Now that I do know liberty, I'll never give it up, and I'll help others to obtain it too."

Tilly hugged Tubman. "Thank you for leading us," she said. She knew what she wanted to do with her newfound liberty. Like Tubman, Tilly would help lead others to freedom.

Vocabulary

despair (page 3) (di spâr´) *n.* A complete loss of hope. *v.* To completely lose hope. Past tense: **despaired** (di spârd´)

creed (page 5) (krēd) *n.* A statement of what a person or group of people believes in.

restrictions (page 6) (ri strik´ shənz) *n.* Plural form of **restriction:** Rule or regulation designed to confine or limit.

overwhelming (page 10) (ō´vər welm´ ing) *adj.* Extreme or great.

clung (page 10) (klung) *v.* Past tense of **cling:** To hold or hold on tightly.

refugees (page 12) (ref´ ū jēz´) *n.* Plural form of **refugee:** A person who flees from a place to find safety or protection.

Comprehension Focus: Drawing Conclusions

1. Why did Eli sit up after he heard the owl hoot five times?

2. What conclusion can you draw about how Tilly felt when she crossed the border of the United States into Canada?